Hazy BLOOM AND THE PET PROJECT

Hazy BLOOM AND THE PET PROJECT

pictures by
Jenn Harney

Jennifer Hamburg

FARRAR STRAUS GIROUX · NEW YORK

Farrar Straus Giroux Books for Young Readers
An imprint of Macmillan Publishing Group, LLC
175 Fifth Avenue, New York, NY 10010

Printed in the United States of America by LSC Communications,
Harrisonburg, Virginia
Designed by Elizabeth H. Clark
First edition, 2018

1 2 3 4 5 6 7 8 9 10

mackids.com

Library of Congress Cataloging-in-Publication Data

Names: Hamburg, Jennifer, author. | Harney, Jenn, illustrator.
Title: Hazy Bloom and the pet project / Jennifer Hamburg ; pictures by
    Jenn Harney.
Description: First edition. | New York : Farrar Straus Giroux, 2018. |
    Summary: "Hazel 'Hazy' Bloom uses her tomorrow power—her ability
    to see visions of things that happen one day in the future—to try
    to convince her parents she's ready for a pet iguana"—Provided by
    publisher. | Identifiers: LCCN 2017023578 (print) | LCCN 2017038541
    (ebook) | ISBN 9780374305000 (ebook) | ISBN 9780374304997
    (hardcover)
Subjects: | CYAC: Extrasensory perception—Fiction. | Family life—
    Fiction. | Schools—Fiction. | Pets—Fiction. | Fund raising—Fiction. |
    Humorous stories.
Classification: LCC PZ7.H1756 (ebook) | LCC PZ7.H1756 Hap 2018 (print) |
    DDC [Fic]—dc23
LC record available at https://lccn.loc.gov/2017023578

Our books may be purchased in bulk for promotional, educational, or
business use. Please contact your local bookseller or Macmillan Cor-
porate and Premium Sales Department at (800) 221-7945, ext. 5442, or
by e-mail at MacmillanSpecialMarkets@macmillan.com.

For Mom and Dad, who I
want to be when I grow up
—Jen

For Owen (it's his turn) and Oliver
(burpmobile designer extraordinaire)
—Jenn

Hazy BLOOM AND THE PET PROJECT

My name is Hazy Bloom, and I can see tomorrow. Not next year, not two weeks from now, tomorrow. Here's how it works: I will be enjoying my day, doing something totally normal, like counting toilet-paper squares, or searching for alien life, or trying to make my own toothpaste, when all of a sudden a "tomorrow vision" will flash into my head of something that's going to happen the next day. Sometimes the vision is crystal clear, and other times it's, well, hazy (ha!). Either way, it's up to me to figure out what the vision means. The good news is, I always get it right.

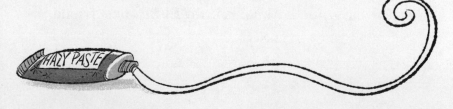

Well, except for the time I turned around all the desks in my classroom as a prank because I was sure we were having a substitute (we weren't). And that other time I snuck out of science lab because I was positive a wagon full of raw eggs was about to plow into a ticket booth (it didn't). Then there was the whole Spring Spectacular catastrophe, where I ruined an acrobatic show in front of the entire school . . .

Okay, fine. I'm not always right. See, my tomorrow power is pretty new. I'm still trying to figure out how it works, how I got it in the first place, and whether I'll be getting any other powers soon, such as dolphin translation or invisibility, which would come in very handy in gym class when we are forced to do push-ups. The point is, I'm getting a new iguana.

Let me back up a bit. It all started this morning, when Elizabeth and I arrived at the school office. Elizabeth Almeida is my BFSB (best friend since birth) and my official "tomorrow power sidekick," which is a job she gave herself but I completely agreed to. Whenever I get a tomorrow vision, Elizabeth is the first to know (besides me, of course). Then she helps me figure out if the vision is about something good (sometimes), bad (most of the time), or wonderful (pretty much never). The point is, if you ever end up with a superpower and need a sidekick, well, you can't call Elizabeth. Because she works with me. Also, I just like having her around because, as my best friend, she's funny, smart, and basically the nicest person in the whole world.

HAZY BLOOM, get over here right now!

She's also a teensy bit bossy.

See, Elizabeth gets a little intense when we have something important to do. And this morning, the two of us had been picked to do the morning announcements at school. As far as Elizabeth was concerned, that was right up there with becoming president or discovering a new planet or holding the door open on the way to recess. In other words, very important.

"Girls, this is *so* exciting!" That was our teacher, Mrs. Agnes. She obviously thought this was important, too, the way she was darting back and forth like we were about to go on national television instead of our school video monitor. "Are you ready? Are you nervous? Do you have everything?"

Elizabeth waved two pieces of paper in her hand. "Everything's right here!" Mrs. Agnes didn't have to worry. Elizabeth was ready. She handed me my paper, which looked like a movie script. It had carefully highlighted lines, some with *ELIZABETH* in front and others with *HAZEL* (my real name) in front. I couldn't help but notice that there were a lot more *ELIZABETH*s than *HAZEL*s. But that was fine with me. She's the performer. I'm the secret superhero.

"Okay, this is it! Places, please!" Mrs. Agnes squealed.

Elizabeth smoothed her shirt and checked that we were standing behind the white line marked on the floor (she was; I was not). Then she nodded professionally to Mrs. Agnes, who pushed a button on the side of the camera. It started blinking.

"It's on!" Mrs. Agnes cried for the whole school to hear as an image of Elizabeth and me flashed onto the video monitors in every classroom. Elizabeth was smiling pleasantly into the camera. She looked happy, comfortable, and confident.

I looked like I was trying to remember when I had last gone to the bathroom.

Mrs. Agnes pointed at us and mouthed, "Action!"

"Good morning and happy Friday, Lipkin Lions!" Elizabeth announced.

In case you're wondering what in the world that means: our school is called Ida Lipkin Elementary School, and our school mascot is the lion. I don't know why it's a lion, because if you ask me, it should be something much more exotic, like the Lipkin Llamas or the Lipkin Lemurs or the Lipkin Squids (who says it has to begin with an *L*?). The point is, I was busy thinking up different animal mascots and totally missed my turn to speak.

"Hazy Bloom, go!" Elizabeth hissed. She jabbed her finger at my paper.

"Oh!" I said, fumbling for my line. I began. "My name is Hazy Bloom. And—"

"And here are today's announcements!" Elizabeth interrupted.

I guess she wanted to say that part.

Elizabeth went on to announce the science-fair finalists. Then she talked about the school clothing drive, which was still accepting donations. Then she reminded everyone to order their yearbooks before the deadline next Friday. Then she performed the song "You're a Grand Old Flag," which I don't think was planned, but it did seem like an effective way for Elizabeth to broadcast her talents to the whole school.

After Elizabeth finished the song, she gestured that it was my turn to speak again. I looked down at my paper.

"And now, the thought of the day." All I had to do was read the quote written on my paper and I'd be finished. Simple. Easy. Done and done.

Except at that very moment, just as I was about to speak . . . a tomorrow vision flashed into my head.

That's how it happens. I'll be doing something perfectly normal, like reading the thought of the day in front of the whole school, when suddenly, I start to feel prickles and goose bumps and my body gets hot and cold at the same time, and then—a picture flashes in my head.

And this picture was of . . . a bright yellow blob. So instead of saying, "A journey of a thousand miles begins with a single step," which was the thought of the day (and an inspiring one, I must say), I said this:

Because that's when I knew I was getting an iguana.

Okay, I know what you're thinking. First, you're thinking, *Did you really need to say, "WooHoo! Yippee! HooYa!" in front of the entire school?* To which the answer is yes, because I was *that* excited. And second, you're thinking, *A blob isn't an iguana*, which obviously I know because I'm not a total birdbrain. But here's what else I know: the yellow blob was almost definitely in the shape of a large animal, and I was 99.9 percent sure that animal was a hippo. And a yellow hippo just *happens* to be the logo for Critter City, a pet shop down the street. And because I'd been begging my parents for an iguana ever since my neighbor Jarrod had a reptile-themed birthday party and I saw an iguana up close and it was love at first sight, I could only conclude they were finally getting me one of my own—tomorrow. I couldn't believe it!

I flashed Elizabeth an ecstatic grin. I couldn't wait to tell her the news. She'd be so happy and excited for me. Or maybe, because she was my best friend and could practically read my mind, she could already *tell* I was getting an iguana and already *was* happy and excited for me.

Then I noticed her expression, which did not

convey *happy* and *excited* as much as *furious* and *about to kill me*. Through gritted teeth, Elizabeth said, "READ. THE. THOUGHT. OF. THE. DAY. NOW."

Perhaps I'd share my iguana news after school.

2

As I had suspected, now that we were in a more relaxed setting—walking home from the bus stop—Elizabeth was delighted to hear my iguana news. As we zigzagged our way down the hill that led to both of our streets, she asked a million questions, like what I would name it, and where it would live, and if she could iguana-sit if I ever had to go somewhere urgent like the doctor's office or Spain. I told her I wasn't planning a trip overseas anytime soon, but if I did, she'd be the first one I'd call. In the meantime, she could play with my iguana whenever she wanted.

After tossing around ideas for names (I liked Marvin, she liked Annabeth Grace), we got to the corner where I turn right and Elizabeth goes straight. I told her I'd call her tomorrow when the iguana arrived. Then I skipped down the street to my house.

When I walked through my front door and dumped my backpack on the floor instead of hanging it in the closet like I'm supposed to because dumping is easier than hanging, the first thing I noticed was that it was quiet. This was weird, because it is never quiet in my house. Between my older brother, Milo, my mom and dad, The Baby, and our dog, Mr. Cheese, there is always some kind of commotion.

"Hello?" I called.

"In here!" Mom's muffled voice yelled back. I walked through the hallway toward The Baby's room and opened the door. A foul smell hit my nose and loud banging attacked my ears. Mom was running around holding a stinky diaper, The Baby was wailing at the top of his lungs, Milo was drumming on the diaper pail, and Mr. Cheese was running in circles, chasing his tail.

I had found the commotion.

"Hazel, please hand me a clean diaper. Not that one; I spilled milk on it. That one over there. Oh, and the baby powder and lotion. Milo, stop drumming and be helpful! No, Hazel, THAT lotion. Not the big bottle, the small bottle. The blue one!"

How about a *Hello and how was your day, and are you excited about your new iguana?* Sheesh.

I picked up a fresh diaper, along with the powder and lotion, and handed them all to Mom. She changed The Baby, then set him down in his crib

and walked over to me. She kissed me on the forehead. "Hi, Hazel Basil. How was your day?"

That was more like it.

"Hi! Fine! Bye!" I said, and ran out of there as fast as I could. The stinky-diaper smell was making me gag.

I went into the kitchen to get a snack (string cheese, six yogurt-covered raisins, and a peach), then beelined to my room. If my new pet was coming tomorrow, I needed to be ready. I couldn't ask my parents to take me to the pet store, because they obviously wanted the iguana to be a surprise or they'd have told me. So it was up to me. And first on the agenda was providing my iguana with a proper home.

I rummaged through my closet, hoping I might find a fully furnished iguana cage somewhere in there, but no such luck. I did, however, find an old shoebox. That would have to do. I cut holes in it so my iguana could breathe. I decorated it inside with some pictures I cut out of magazines so he could look at some art while he was in there. I filled a paper cup full of water in case he was thirsty, then I put some of Mr. Cheese's squeaky toys inside in case he wanted to play. Then I realized he'd need food. I went to the kitchen and found some salami, but then I remembered from my reptile research that iguanas are herbivores and prefer fruits and leafy greens to lunch meat. I put the salami back and took out a head of lettuce, green beans, and a cut-up plum. I put them in a bowl, stuck the bowl in the shoebox, then placed the entire habitat near my window so he'd get enough sun (important for iguanas!). I stepped back and surveyed my work.

Honestly? If I were an iguana, I'd totally want to live there.

Now I just had to wait until tomorrow.

3

At 9:45 the next morning, a giant truck rolled down the street to our house, and the first thing I noticed, even from far away, was that right there painted on the side of the truck was the big yellow hippo from my vision. *Wow*, I thought.

Door-to-door service! This was even better than I'd imagined.

But as the truck got closer, I noticed that the yellow hippo wasn't a hippo at all—it was a porcupine. Then I noticed that above the porcupine, in fancy cursive writing, it did not say *Critter City*, like it was supposed to. Instead, it said, *Tagallino Building Supplies*. Well, that was weird. I mean, I'd heard of them before and knew they sold lumber and wood and other stuff I didn't care about, because between you and me, there is nothing more boring than lumber. I thought it was a little odd that they also sold iguanas, but hey, it's their company, they can do what they want.

Two men climbed out and started unloading stacks of wood from the back of the truck. Then together they unloaded long wooden beams and sheets of plywood and other materials and started carrying it into our house. I wasn't sure what any of this had to do with an

iguana. Maybe we were going to build it a giant house, which was exciting to imagine.

"This way, this way. Straight to the back," Dad was saying to the men, looking rather ecstatic. *To the back where?* I thought. Then Milo appeared in the doorway.

"Awesome! It's here!"

What's here?

As the men carried the lumber through the front door, my entire family seemed to be beside themselves with excitement. I couldn't tell who was happier: Milo, Mom, Dad, The Baby, or Mr. Cheese, who must have thought it had something to do with him by the way he was wildly wagging his tail. You know who wasn't happy? Me. Because I was busy wondering what in the world was happening.

"Last door on the right," Dad said. Milo's room. The men turned right and headed down the hallway.

"Can someone please tell me what's going on?" I demanded.

"What's going on is . . . I'm getting a new loft bed, Stink Face!" Milo shouted.

First of all, that was no language to use in front of the deliverymen, who were guests. Second of all, I was slowly, dreadfully beginning to understand what was happening: My vision hadn't been about a pet store delivering me an iguana. It had been about a lumberyard delivering lumber for Milo's loft bed. I had two immediate thoughts: 1. I hate Milo, and 2. Why would the logo for a lumber company be a porcupine, because that makes absolutely no sense, for real live?

After tipping the deliverymen, Dad walked them out, then he and Mom headed back to Milo's room.

Or they tried to, until I jumped in front of them, blocking their way.

"Hazel, what is it?" Mom said.

I decided to start by calmly asking some questions.

It's possible I didn't express myself the way I had planned.

Dad raised his eyebrows. "Hazel, is there something you'd like to discuss?"

"Why does Milo get a loft bed? Why don't I get one? How come you didn't tell me? Why does he get everything? Where's my iguana?"

My parents seemed baffled by my explosion of questions, especially the last one, but Mom calmly explained that she and Dad had made a deal with Milo: If he did all of his chores without fail for a month and showed that he was responsible, he would get a loft bed. Which led me to say, "Milo? *Responsible?* Ha!"

Except now that I thought about it, I realized that Milo *had* been hanging up his backpack after school. And I kind of remembered him clearing the dinner table a

lot more. Also, now that I looked around his room, except for the enormous pile of wood on the floor that The Baby was currently drooling all over, it did seem bizarrely clean and not as stinky as usual.

Still, I wasn't going to stand for this. "Just so you know, I'm responsible, too. I'm the most re-sponsiblest person on the planet!" It was true! I always cleared my plate (well, almost always). I kept my room spotless (except for the massive heap of clothes on the floor). I fed my fish every single solitary—

(Actually, when was the last time . . .)

"Be right back," I said, and bolted to my room.

Phew, my fish were fine. They just looked hungry. I sprinkled a few extra flakes in the tank, but not too many, because that wouldn't be safe. See? Responsible!

Then I tripped on the heap of clothes on my

floor and dropped the food container, causing
fish-food flakes to scatter everywhere, which
Mr. Cheese started lapping up like it was a doggie
version of an ice cream sundae. By the time I
dragged him away from the flakes and found the
cap to the container (that he had tried to eat, too),
then shook out my clothes because they smelled
like an aquarium, for real live, I was exhausted.

4

Apparently, Dad had decided he was going to build Milo's loft bed all by himself, which was an interesting choice considering it once took him three days to figure out how to hang a shower curtain. I mean, don't get me wrong—Dad is great at a lot of things. He is a master crossword-puzzle solver. A marvelous scrambled-eggs maker. An impressive

YYOOODELLLEEᶜHEEHOOOₒₒₒ

yodeler (a recent and delight-ful discovery). But building a loft bed from scratch? I had my doubts. Still, he seemed determined.

For the rest of the weekend, Dad and Milo made a racket getting everything ready for building, which included:

- clearing space for the new bed
- laying out the materials
- redrawing the plans they'd already drawn
- laying out more materials
- testing every single power tool known to man
- deciding they needed to go to the hardware store for more tools and materials

As for me, I chose to spend my weekend sulking, moping, and imagining ways to get back at Milo.

On Sunday afternoon, I was lying on my

(not loft) bed picturing an iguana pooping in Milo's shoes when Mom popped her head into my room. I rolled away from her. I was in no mood to talk.

"Phone call for you, Hazy," she said.

"Tell Elizabeth I'll call her later," I grumbled.

"It's not Elizabeth. It's Aunt Jenna."

I sat up.

5

Do you know what it's like to be excited, nervous, scared, and itchy all at the same time? Because that's how I suddenly felt. To be fair, the itchy part was just because I had gotten some fish flakes inside my sweater. But the rest of it was because of Aunt Jenna. I was finally going to talk to her about my tomorrow power. Or rather, *our* tomorrow power.

Because I think Aunt Jenna has it, too.

Let me explain. Last month, Aunt Jenna came to visit for a week. While she was here, she did a whole bunch of weird stuff—not weird like when Milo sniffs his feet after he takes off his sneakers, or weird like when The Baby says "meow" to the dog—I mean weird as in this: during the entire week, everything Aunt Jenna gave me or told me about was something I ended up needing *the very next day.* As in, tomorrow. The craziest part is that I didn't even figure out she had tomorrow power until after she'd gone, so I never got to talk to her about it. Since then, I'd called her and left messages, but so far I hadn't heard back. Until now.

Sure, I wished she had called me sooner, but it's like I always say: *it's better to be late than to never show up at the farm.* Actually, I've never said that, but I'm pretty sure someone has in this type of situation. Whatever it means.

I took the phone from Mom, my heart beating out of my chest. This was it. I was finally going to hear Aunt Jenna admit she had tomorrow power, just like me. I'd already imagined that together we'd be a team of doom-preventing

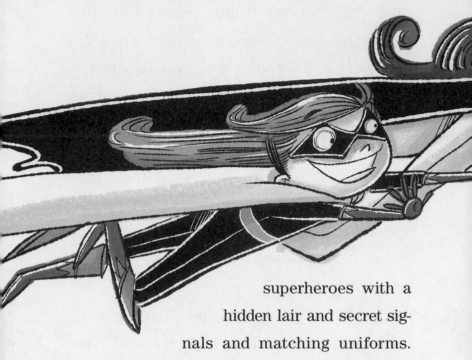

superheroes with a hidden lair and secret signals and matching uniforms. I'd wondered if she'd be okay with purple.

I put the phone to my ear, first making sure Mom was far down the hall. "Hello?"

"Hazy Bloom!" Aunt Jenna chirped. "I am *so sorry* I didn't call back sooner, but I've been away on a work trip." She continued, "Do you want to hear the funniest thing?"

If it wasn't about tomorrow power, I did not, but I said, "Sure."

So Aunt Jenna launched into a long story about a cornfield, a turtle, and a twice-baked potato that I very patiently listened to and even laughed at a little (the potato part was kind of funny).

After her story, she asked me how school was going, what the weather was like, and if I was doing anything fun this weekend.

I answered all of her questions, then felt it was time to get to the point. "What about . . . you know . . ."

I trailed off, hoping she would finish the sentence.

"I'm sorry, I don't know," she replied. "What about what?"

I covered my mouth and whispered into the phone, like I was in a spy movie. *"Our tomorrow power."*

"Our what? I'm sorry, Hazy Bloom, I'm not sure what you mean."

Well, that was a curveball. I tried a different approach. "Aunt Jenna, is there anything special you want to tell me? About you? And me? And preventing doom?"

"Doom? Well, I've started planting an herb garden, but I accidentally put the oregano in the parsley section and the mint where the basil should be, if that's what you mean! I'm also growing rosemary and cilantro and . . ."

Aunt Jenna rattled on, naming herbs I'd never heard of, but I was NI (not interested).

Number one, if there is anything more boring than lumber, it's herbs.

Number two, why was she saying she didn't have tomorrow power?

In the background, I heard Aunt Jenna's doorbell ring.

"Oh! My friends are here to see the garden. Call me again soon, okay?"

That was *it*?

"Oh, and Hazy Bloom?" From her voice, it seemed like something had just occurred to her.

"Yes?"

"Remember to drink water at school, okay? Love you!" And she hung up.

So much for discussing matching uniforms.

I was seriously confused. Why would Aunt Jenna say she didn't know what I meant? *Did* she know what I meant? Or was I completely wrong about Aunt Jenna having tomorrow power after all?

Also, why was she talking about water?

I flopped back onto my bed to continue my sulking-and-moping marathon, especially given the pointless conversation I'd just had. Outside my door, I could hear Milo on the phone, telling his friend about his cool new bed, which once again reminded me of the iguana I wasn't getting. I considered opening my door and hurling my pillow at his head, but I stopped at the last minute because a) I really liked that pillow, and b) I suddenly realized *exactly* how I could get my iguana. I just had to prove to my parents that I was the most responsible kid on the planet. I could totally do it! And I'd start by picking up the heap of clothes on my floor.

But before I got through a single layer of shirts (so *that's* where my sparkly mermaid hoodie was!), I was interrupted by the familiar sensation of prickles and goose bumps, and next thing I knew, I was staring at a series of letters and symbols that made no sense at all:

Luke was doing his chair-kicking thing again. Every time I'd write something on my fractions worksheet, he'd kick the back of my seat and make my pencil skid across the page. As a result, my equation looked like this:

$$\frac{4}{6} + \frac{1}{6} =$$

Luke does this kind of thing for one reason and one reason only: to be annoying. This is why I call him "Mapefrl," which stands for "most annoying person ever, for real live."

I've known Mapefrl since kindergarten and

had been sure he couldn't get any more annoying. But it turns out, due to the chair-kicking thing, he could. Who knew?

"All right, everyone. Papers forward!" Mrs. Agnes said.

I quickly erased my scribble scrawl caused by Mapefrl and handed off my paper. I thought about complaining to Mrs. Agnes and requesting a new seat assignment, which shouldn't have been difficult since they do it on airplanes all the time—but then I thought better of it. The truth was, I didn't want to waste time dealing with Mapefrl when I had more important things to do, like studying my hand. Because that's where I'd written the series of weird letters that had appeared in my vision the day before. I had meant to write them on a piece of paper, but I couldn't find one on account of my room looking like a hurricane had blown through (I hadn't gotten very far with the heap of clothes). So I ended up grabbing a marker and writing on the back of my hand as neatly and clearly as possible, then made sure not to use that hand for *anything* until the next day, which, let me tell you, is not easy when you're doing your business on the toilet.

The good news is, twelve hours later (or ½ of one day, if you're practicing your fractions), I had managed to not smudge the word at all. It was still as clear as day. And it still made absolutely no sense. Total gibberish. Luckily, right after math we have free time. Now was my chance to figure it out.

Then, as usual, Mrs. Agnes ruined everything.

"Instead of free time today, we're going to discuss our ideas for the Third-Grade FUNd-raising Challenge!"

So, about this FUNdraising Challenge. It was a big deal. Each of the three third-grade classes would be spending the next few weeks coming up with a unique and original FUNd-raising event, planning that event, then hosting the event for the entire school, and when it was all over, the class that raised the most money would be declared the FUNdraising Challenge winner. The point is, it didn't seem that fun, so I would recommend they change the name.

Clearly, Mrs. Agnes did not agree, because

she was now excitedly wheeling out her white-board, which she only uses to write important things like "Spelling quiz tomorrow!" or "Field trip forms!" or "Be inquisitive!" which, if you ask me, is a hard thing to do when it's being demanded of you. In any case, while Mrs. Agnes was getting out five different-colored dry-erase markers, Mapefrl kicked my chair again, so I whirled around and swatted at him.

"Hazel! Luke! Please behave," Mrs. Agnes scolded. "We have a lot to talk about today and I don't want any distractions."

I scowled at Luke and turned back around.

Mrs. Agnes gleefully wrote "FUNdraiser" on her whiteboard, then turned to the class. "So! Who has ideas for *our* class fundraiser?"

"Me! I have ideas! I've put together a list and made copies for everyone. I'll hand them out!"

I'll give you one guess who that was. Yup. Elizabeth. She jumped up from her chair and started handing out sheets of paper to each row. Mrs. Agnes looked a little bummed, probably because now she had nothing to write on her whiteboard.

I took a sheet from Elizabeth and read through her ideas:

Elizabeth's GREAT FUNDRAISER IDEAS!!
☆ Talent Show
☆ Sing-along
☆ Skit Night
☆ Vaudeville Musical
☆ Magic Show
☆ Interpretive Dance
☆ Comedy Improvisation
☆ Shakespearean Monologue Competition
♡ -Elizabeth

If it occurred to you that everything on this list was alike in exactly one way, you'd be right: they were all opportunities for Elizabeth to perform. I, for one, was perfectly fine with any of these ideas, especially the magic show, because I have a card trick that would blow your mind, for real live.

Unfortunately, the rest of the class didn't feel the same way. Over the next five minutes, everyone discussed Elizabeth's ideas one by one. And by "discussed," I mean "said no to."

I could tell she was disappointed. But not as disappointed as Mrs. Agnes, who still had nothing to write on her whiteboard. Soon it was almost lunchtime and we had exactly zero ideas.

Mrs. Agnes said to take a quick break and then we'd continue.

I was stretching my legs when I suddenly remembered what Aunt Jenna had said about drinking water. At first I thought about ignor-

ing her advice because I a) still didn't understand why she said it, b) was still a little mad at
her for not having tomorrow power after all,
and c) wasn't thirsty. But after a moment, I
changed my mind. I'm not sure why. I just felt
like I should do it.

I went to the classroom sink, grabbed a
paper cup, and filled it up. As I took a sip, I
stared in the mirror above the faucet. And that's
when I saw the reflection of my hand, and the
gibberish that was written on it. Except now I
could see that it wasn't gibberish at all. It was a
word—or words—
in reverse. And in
the mirror, I could
read them perfectly.

"Pet . . . day,"
I said to myself
slowly. "Pet. Day.
Pet Day."

Derrick, whose desk is right next to the sink, looked over his shoulder. "Pet Day? That's a great idea!" Then he called to the class, "Hey, everyone, Hazy has an idea for the fundraiser!"

I swirled around. "Wait, what?" I stammered.

"Ooh, what is it?" said Lila, Derrick's twin sister.

"It's nothing. I—"

"Yeah, what?" May asked.

"No really, I was just talking to my—"

"Pet Day!" Derrick practically screamed.

Everyone went quiet. Then they all looked at each other. And erupted in cheers.

"Yes! Pet Day!"

"That's it!"

"I love it!"

"That's our FUNdraiser!"

Before I knew it, the entire class was clustered around me, ideas gushing like water from a fire hydrant a dog had just peed on and accidentally set off.

"We can have a pet wash!"

"And a pet fashion show!"

"And pet treats!"

"And pet portraits!"

"Yes, pet portraits!"

Mrs. Agnes jumped

in. "It does sound like fun. I could bring Pookie!"

I guessed Pookie was her pet. With that name, I hoped it wasn't a human, for its own sake.

As my classmates ($^{22}\!/_{23}$ of them, to be exact) chattered nonstop to me about all the fun pet-related things we could do, I glanced nervously at Elizabeth, hoping she'd come to my rescue. But she looked deep in thought. Maybe even a little upset. Was she mad that everyone was excited about my idea and not any of hers?

I cleared my throat. "What do *you* think about Pet Day, Elizabeth?" I asked loudly, so the whole class would give her the attention she deserved.

"I think . . . I think . . ." She paused. "I think you'll need entertainment. And that entertainment will be me!"

Leave it to Elizabeth! She's the

only person I know who can find a way to perform at an event featuring animals.

After a quick classroom vote, it was settled, and Mrs. Agnes wrote in big block letters on her whiteboard: PET DAY! I imagine that must have felt very satisfying.

I was satisfied, too. Now that I had solved my tomorrow vision, suggested a brilliant idea for our fundraiser, and pretty much booked a gig for Elizabeth, I could move on to other things, like making a plan to keep my iguana away from predatory birds (an iguana's worst enemy).

But then the worst thing in the entire world happened, for real live. I suddenly heard Mrs. Agnes saying that we'd need a team leader for Pet Day, and then my classmates were saying things like "It was her idea" and "She suggested it" and "She should do it!"

Then Mrs. Agnes said this: "Well, then, it's

settled. Class, your team leader for our FUNd-raiser is . . . Hazel Bloom!"

I could not believe this.

Mrs. Agnes wrote my name on the white-board. Everyone clapped. Except for Mapefrl, who kicked my chair again.

I imagined I was an iguana, which are known to use their tails to punch their enemies. That would have felt very good right about then.

At lunch, even though Mom had packed my favorite sandwich—cream cheese, jelly, and pickles on wheat bread with the crusts cut off—I wasn't hungry because I was freaking out about my new job as team leader.

"How am I going to do this?" I wailed to my friends. "I've never been a team leader. I've never even been a regular leader!"

"You've been line leader," Lila reminded me.

That was true.

"But she led the line to the playground instead of art as a joke and got us all in trouble," said Derrick

That was also true.

I sighed and picked at my sandwich. "I don't want to be in charge of the fundraiser. All I want to do is go home and make a hammock for Fred."

"Who's Fred?" Derrick asked.

"My iguana. Who now I'll never get," I said with a sigh. I had decided "Fred" was the perfect name: strong, but sensitive.

My friends glanced at each other. They knew how badly I wanted an iguana, because it's pretty much all I'd been talking about lately. In fact, they were probably sick of hearing about it. But I didn't care. At that moment I felt like complaining, so that's exactly what I did. For the next minute (or approximately $\frac{1}{30}$ of lunch period), I went on to grumble that because of this team-leader situation, I now wouldn't have time to show my parents how responsible I am, and since that was the only way they would ever agree to get me an iguana, I could pretty much assume that I'd never get the pet of my dreams for as long as I live. I followed all of this with a dramatic "woe is me" sigh, just to make sure they understood my despair.

Elizabeth turned to me, her eyes full of concern. I expected her to say something comforting and optimistic to make me feel better.

Instead, I got this: "What happened to Annabeth Grace?"

"Pardon me?"

"Your iguana's name. I really think it's better than Fred."

Seriously? I'd just poured my heart out in the middle of the lunchroom and this was what she was focusing on?

Lila and Derrick started oohing and aahing

about what a great name Annabeth Grace was, which did not help my mood, and then they all started blathering about Pet Day again, while I tuned them out so I could concentrate on being miserable.

"Hazy Bloom, are you listening?"

"No thanks."

"HAZY BLOOM!" Elizabeth looked at me. "I was *saying* that if you are in charge of the fundraiser . . . and if we *win* the fundraising challenge . . . then your parents will see that you're the most responsible person on the planet! And they'll get you an iguana!"

And there you have it, folks. My genius best friend.

A slow smile spread across my face.

She was one hundred percent right. What would I do without her?

It turns out I wouldn't have to find out, because she immediately appointed herself "vice team leader," which I don't think is an actual job, but hey, I needed all the help I could get. Especially since I still had no idea what a team leader was supposed to do.

VICE
TEAM
LEADER

8

That night, after I finished my homework, I made a plan. Like it or not (not), I had been chosen as team leader for Pet Day, and like it or not (not), I had an obligation to fulfill my team-leader duties. I would begin by going to the family room and watching television for the rest of the night.

I realize this may not sound like a team-leader kind of plan, but my thinking went like this: a team leader needs to be relaxed and calm so she can do team-leader-y things, and I was most definitely not relaxed and calm. Watching television, however, would help me *become* relaxed and calm, especially if the home-shopping channel had a good show on. I hoped they were showing those toaster ovens that can make four pizzas at once.

I flipped on the TV and settled onto the couch. I was feeling better already.

Then that feeling was destroyed by the most awful noise I'd ever heard.

What in the world?

I leaped off the couch and sped down the hallway, the noise getting louder and more horrible by the second.

I entered Milo's room. Milo was steadying a worktable while Dad attempted to saw a piece of wood. They were both wearing giant, goofy protective goggles. On the floor, a bunch of wood pieces were scattered among the tools and other materials.

"Dabagradacha!"

Oh, and The Baby was there. In a porta-crib far away from the dangerous spinning power saw. He was wearing goggles, too.

After finishing the cut, Dad turned the saw off and looked at me.

"Oh, hiya, Hazel Basil! We're just getting under way with Milo's loft bed."

I surveyed the room, which looked like a war zone. How all of those pieces of junk

were going to turn into a loft bed was beyond me.

Dad picked up two wood pieces. "All righty, if my calculations are correct, these two should be the exact same size."

He held them side by side. One was about three inches shorter than the other (which is $3/12$ if you measure in feet).

"Huh," Dad said.

"Are you sure you know what you're doing?" I asked.

"Oh, definitely!" he said. Then he knocked into the worktable.

"Dad!" Milo yelped as he and I rushed to grab it before it crashed to the floor.

"Whoopsy daisy!" Dad said. Then he secured his goofy goggles and went right back to work.

So much for relaxing.

I went into the kitchen to do the dishes, which, trust me, surprised me as much as anyone. But I figured it was an opportunity to distract myself from the deafening noise *and* get in some responsibility points while I was at it.

I picked up a dish and it immediately slipped from my hand to the floor, where it smashed into pieces.

Broken dish: 1. Horrible noises: 2. Good things that happened to me today: 0.

9

I absolutely hate to admit this, but I'm going to give it to you straight: I kind of avoided Elizabeth after school the next day. It's just that ever since yesterday, when I'd accidentally come up with our brilliant (not)FUNdraising idea, all she (and my entire class) had been yapping about was Pet Day, Pet Day, Pet Day. It had been less than twenty-four hours, and I was tired of it already.

Luckily for me, Milo was staying late after school for a science project and I knew Mom was coming to pick him up. So when the

dismissal bell rang, instead of heading to the bus, where I knew I'd face more Pet Day jibber-jabber from Elizabeth, I hustled to the library.

I pushed open the door to find the librarian, Mrs. Fowler, pushing a cart of books across the floor.

"Hello, Hazel! How nice to see you."

Mrs. Fowler was the complete opposite of Mrs. Agnes: soft-spoken, sweet, and had never put me in time-out. I liked her. But when she asked me what I was doing there, I couldn't exactly say I was avoiding my best friend, so I replied, "I'm looking for a book about iguanas."

"Wonderful! Follow me to the reptile section," she said.

It turned out the reptile section consisted of two worn-out books about geckos, a magazine featuring turtles, and a picture book called *Can a Crocodile Cluck?* with the front cover ripped in half.

Mrs. Fowler's reptile section needed some serious work.

I sighed and plopped down at a table to do my homework until it was time for Mom to pick up Milo and me out front. It had been a long day and I was ready to go home.

. . . . .

I should have stayed at the library. Because as soon as we entered our house, it was clear that Dad had moved on from the buzz saw to the power drill, which made a different, even more horrible noise than before.

WHIRRRRR. WHIRRRRR. WHIRRRRR.

With my hands over my ears, I peered into Milo's room to see how close Dad was to finishing this ridiculous project. By the looks of things, he didn't seem very close, since nothing in there was looking even remotely like a bed yet. What a mess. The only upside to all this ruckus was that, among the items in the war zone, I spotted a giant strip of Bubble Wrap, which is kind of the best invention ever (besides a four-pizza toaster oven). I swiped it and hotfooted out of there.

I was popping away in the living room when The Baby waddled over and tried to grab the entire piece from me, to which I said, "Hands off, bub. That's mine."

The Baby said, "Slageerat!"

which I could only interpret

as "Ha! Nice try, tall person, but I'm a baby, and when I see something that crinkles and pops like crazy, by golly, I'm not letting that opportunity pass me by!" Then he grabbed it again.

Annoyed, I picked up The Baby and was removing him from the Bubble Wrap area when suddenly, I felt the tingles and goose bumps. And then, all of a sudden, it wasn't The Baby I was holding. It was Mrs. Agnes. Now, before you freak out like I almost did, The Baby didn't *actually* turn into Mrs. Agnes, because that would be

completely bananas. I was having a tomorrow vision of Mrs. Agnes . . . holding something round in her hand and smiling. I'm not sure what she was holding or why she was smiling about it, but the point is, by the time the vision was gone, The Baby had squirmed from my arms and was messing with my Bubble Wrap again. Argh!

I delivered the little rascal to my mom and was heading to my room to figure out my vision when the doorbell rang. It was Elizabeth.

Uh-oh.

"Hi!" I said as cheerfully as possible, trying to pretend I hadn't been avoiding her for the last several hours.

"Why weren't you on the bus?" she demanded.

I thought quickly. "I had my violin lesson."

"You don't take violin."

"You don't know everything about me!"

"Yes, I do."

"Oh, fine." She had me. I decided to come clean. "Look, the real reason is—"

"Oh, never mind," she said, waving her arm. Then she smiled. "I brought you something."

Frankly, if it wasn't more Bubble Wrap, I wasn't interested.

But then she held out something, as proud as could be. "Ta-da!"

It was a notebook.

"What's this?" I asked suspiciously.

"It's your new Ultimate Pet Day Planning Guide. Written, designed, and color-coded by me!"

I stared at her.

So she said, "Trust me, you need this."

"I do?"

"Yes!" Elizabeth pushed past me and sat down at the kitchen table as she continued to talk. "Pet Day is *one week from Saturday*! That means you have less than two weeks left to plan! Don't you want to run the best fundraiser ever? Yes! And raise the most money? Yes! And impress your parents so they'll get you an iguana? Yes, you want all of those things!"

In case you missed it, Elizabeth just asked and answered all of her own questions. She does this when she feels it's easier than talking to a whole other person.

I sat down next to her and opened the notebook. There was a calendar, a "To-Do" list, an "Urgent To-Do" list, a section for notes, and a motivational thought for each day. Elizabeth then proceeded to take me through each and every page, pointing to a never-ending list of things I needed to do:

"These are the items for people to donate. This is a list of food to be ordered. These are the treats we need for the goody bags. This is the phone number for the pet-portrait artist—who is my mom's friend—but you need to call her AS SOON AS POSSIBLE before she books another event. Here's a list of art supplies we need for the posters . . ." On and on and on she went.

My head began to spin. "I have to do all these things?"

"Of course not. Everyone in the class will help."

"Phew."

"But you're in charge of making sure it all gets done."

"Oh."

"And sticking to the schedule."

"Okay . . ."

"And fixing any problems that come up along the way."

Just great. I glanced out of the corner of my eye at the planning guide, then quickly looked away. Who knew a bunch of paper and notebook tabs could make me so anxious?

"Now, let's go over the budget!" Elizabeth said ecstatically.

I needed to change the subject, and fast.

"Hazy Bloom, are you paying attention?"

"I had another vision."

Elizabeth immediately set down the planning guide, and I smiled. Because if there's one thing my BFSB cares more about than her own brilliant ideas, it's my tomorrow visions. She is my sidekick, after all.

"Talk to me," she said, leaning forward, her chin in her hands.

I told her about Mrs. Agnes and the round . . . something that she was holding.

"Something round, huh . . ." She tapped her pencil against her cheek. "Was it a penny?"

I thought about it, then shook my head. "No, bigger."

"A Hula-Hoop?"

"Smaller."

"A bicycle wheel?"

"Why would she be holding a bicycle wheel?" I said.

"I don't know!" Elizabeth sighed. "We need more information. Did you see *anything* else?"

I squeezed my eyes shut, trying to remember. Again, I saw Mrs. Agnes smiling . . . and . . . about to take a bite? And wait—were those chocolate chips?

My eyes popped open. "She's going to eat something!" I gave Elizabeth a knowing smile. "Something with chocolate chips . . ."

"Why would a bicycle wheel have chocolate chips?"

I threw my arms in the air. "It's *not* a bicycle wheel! It's a cookie! A chocolate chip cookie!"

Elizabeth pursed her lips thoughtfully. "A vision of Mrs. Agnes eating a cookie. *Hmmmmmmm.*"

My thoughts exactly.

Since we weren't getting anywhere, Elizabeth suggested we get back to the planning guide and talk about my vision later. "Now where were we . . . Oh yeah. First on the To-Do list: promote team spirit!"

I sighed again. I didn't want to talk about team spirit, for real live.

But Elizabeth was already off and running. "It's very important to promote team spirit and get everyone excited about Pet Day. Do you understand? Yes, of course you do," she asked and answered all by herself.

"How do I promote team spirit?" I asked nervously.

"Lots of ways! You can give a speech, or make up a cheer, or hand out buttons, or bake something for the whole class to eat like—"

Elizabeth stopped talking, because suddenly we had the exact same thought at the exact same moment. Round . . . small . . . chocolate chips . . .

"Chocolate chip cookies!" we said together.

Vision solved. We were getting good at this superhero-sidekick thing.

10

The next morning, after catching a ride to school with Dad, I strutted into my classroom holding a giant plastic-wrapped platter of freshly baked chocolate chip cookies. Well, actually they weren't freshly baked because I'd made them the night before, after Elizabeth went home. And they didn't have chocolate chips, because we didn't have any, so I had to use frozen blueberries. Also, Mom kept the flour, sugar, salt, and every other white powdery ingredient known to man in clear Tupperware containers, so it took me a while to find what I needed because they all looked exactly the same. And by that time I was so frustrated that I just kind of dumped the stuff together to get it over with.

Also, I didn't really strut into the classroom. I kind of baby-stepped across the floor until I reached my desk so I wouldn't drop anything. But still. I had cookies. And if I do say so myself, they looked delicious.

"Hazel, what a nice surprise!" Mrs. Agnes said, admiring the platter. "What's the occasion?"

I told her the occasion was team spirit. So let's get this cookie party started!

But Mrs. Agnes said we'd have to wait until later in the morning to eat the cookies, which led me to wonder aloud who exactly invented the rule that cookies can only be eaten after a certain hour, because frankly, they taste the same no matter what time it is, for real live. The point is, Mrs. Agnes still made us wait until morning break. Then it was cookie time.

I took out the platter and gave a cookie to everyone in the class ($23/25$ of my cookies, because I had exactly two left). Then I offered one to Mrs. Agnes.

"Why, thank you!" she said, holding the cookie and smiling. I remembered that smile. From my vision, of course. I also remembered the next part of my vision, when she took a giant bite.

Then, in an unexpected twist, she spit the entire thing out. Cookie crumbs and blueberry

bits sprayed across her desk. I made a mental note to donate some napkins to the class.

"Mrs. Agnes? Are you okay?" I asked as she wiped her mouth. Before I could hear her answer, I turned to see everyone else spitting out their cookies, too.

"Ick!"

"These are terrible!"

"Something is *wrong* with these!"

Wrong? Now, to be honest, I hadn't tried the cookies yet. It had looked like I might not have enough for everyone, so I skipped the taste test. Also, I'm not crazy

about blueberries. But I had to know what was going on. I picked up the last cookie and took a nibble. *Blech!* It turned out the blueberries were the least of my problems. Because remember all those clear  containers in the pantry? Well, apparently the one I thought was sugar wasn't sugar. It was salt.

First of all, I was going to buy my mom some labels, because this clear-container stuff was ridiculous. Second of all, why in the world did my vision show Mrs. Agnes *before* she ate the cookie and not *after*, when she was spitting it out, which, although disgusting, would have been a much more helpful vision for me to have? I was so mad about my tomorrow vision giving me such useless information that when Mapefrl kicked the back of my chair during math, I turned around and kicked his chair right back. Except I missed his chair and got his shin.

He howled.

Ten seconds later, Mapefrl and I were ushered into the hallway by Mrs. Agnes, given a lecture about our "childish" behavior, and then informed that from now on we'd be forced to *sit next to each other at lunch until we figured out how to get along.* If that's not torture, I don't know what is. Except perhaps eating one of my cookies.

11

Lunch was a nightmare. Actually, it was worse than a nightmare, and, trust me, I've had some bad nightmares (including a recent one where The Baby grew fangs and gnawed his high chair in half). This was a nightmare because I was now sitting next to Mapefrl, and in case you were wondering, we were not figuring out how to get along. Instead, he was drawing a comic strip about a superhero named Burp Man. Who burped. A lot. As Mapefrl kept demonstrating.

So gross.

Even worse, word had gotten around about my horrible blueberry-salt cookies. Most kids were nice about it, saying they were sorry it had happened. But I saw a few other kids snickering as they walked past, which was not helping my bad mood.

By recess, just when I thought I couldn't handle another cookie comment, Summer Beckett skipped over to where Elizabeth and I were standing. I didn't know Summer too well, but I did know that she was a) also in third grade, b) named after a season, and c) the team leader for Mr. Plinker's class fundraiser. It was also my impression that she was a little bit snooty.

"Hi, Hazy," Summer said.

"I DIDN'T KNOW IT WAS SALT!" I shouted back.

She looked confused. Then she handed me a flyer. "For our fundraiser," she said.

There were three third-grade classes in all. I knew that Ms. Simone's class was doing a car wash for their fundraiser. We, of course, were doing Pet Day, and even though I didn't *exactly* think of it myself, I was pretty sure it was the most creative idea of all three classes put together. Until I looked at Summer's flyer.

ALOHA! JOIN US FOR THE FIRST-EVER LIPKIN LUAU!

Okay, that was a very close second.

"You're having a luau?" Elizabeth asked, her eyes wide with envy.

"Yep," Summer chirped. "It's going to be amaaaaaazing."

Well, she didn't have to rub it in. Sheesh.

"Oh yeah?" I piped in. "Well, our fundraiser is Pet Day, and it's going to be *more* amazing. We have everything planned already. EVERY-

THING!" I'm not sure why I added that part, but I can tell you it led to several follow-up questions.

"Really? When is it?"

"I'm not quite sure—"

"Where will it be?"

"We're still trying to—"

"What's going to be there?"

"Uhhhhhhhh—"

Wasn't it time to go back inside?

Summer gave me a funny look and said, "Sounds like you haven't figured *everything* out."

She turned to go, but not before handing me something in a napkin. "Oh, I made cookies for our class. You know, for team spirit. We had extras."

Elizabeth jutted out her chin. "No, thank you. We don't want your—"

"I'll take one!" I interrupted. Even in this circumstance, turning down an actual, no-salt chocolate chip cookie just seemed unnecessary.

Though I hate to admit, it was the most delicious chocolate chip cookie I'd ever had.

12

Mom was mad, and I could tell this because she was yelling at the sink. I don't know why she takes out her anger on inanimate objects, but when she's in this kind of mood, I don't ask questions. What made it worse, however, was today she was mad because of me.

Apparently, after I made my disastrous cookies the night before, I'd forgotten to put away the milk, so it spoiled. Mom discovered this after I'd left for school, and The Baby had nothing to drink, which resulted in a thirty-minute tantrum (from The Baby, not my mom). Then, The Baby found the butter (which I also forgot to put away) and smushed it all over his head. Mom had been trying to get it out of his hair all day, with no luck.

I'd wondered why The Baby's hair looked so shiny.

When Mom finally turned her famous laser glare at me, she said that not putting things away after I used them is irresponsible behavior, and because of my actions, she now has a baby who keeps smushing things on his head to see if they'll stick.

I told Mom I was sorry and offered to drive to the store to buy more milk and butter, which I kind of knew was impossible on account of my being nine. Also, just to be clear, this was definitely not helping with the iguana situation. Thinking things couldn't get any worse, I slinked away before Mom could discover any other horrible things I'd done.

I was wrong.

WHIRRRRR. WHIRRRRR. WHIRRRRR.

Dad's drill of destruction.

Why was our house so small? For once, I wanted some peace and quiet. I tried The Baby's empty room but couldn't find anywhere to sit (except the diaper pail, and trust me, you didn't want to sit on that). Next I tried Mom's office, but she had been cleaning her desk and had an enormous stack of papers on her chair. After attempting the bathtub, the back porch, and the attic (which seemed okay until I remembered what Milo had once said about a ghost who lived up there and ate kids whose names began with *H*), I found the only place where I could get away from the noise: the laundry room. I hopped up on the washing machine and criss-

crossed my legs, ready to stay
there forever.

Except after four and a half
minutes, I was bored out of
my mind. I looked around.
Maybe I could do some
laundry? I mean, that
would be a huge help for
Mom and Dad, and that meant I could prove
that I was . . . *ding ding ding!* Responsible!
There was even a basket of dirty clothes sitting
on the floor, just waiting to be washed. So, with
this genius plan, I spent the next hour washing,
drying, and even folding the clothes, including
a wrap dress of Mom's, which, let me tell you,
was no walk in the park.

When I was done, I stuck my head out the
laundry room door and yelled to my family,
"Clean clothes! Come and get 'em . . . while
they're hot!" I believe that's what you say about

baked goods and not laundry, but I couldn't help it. I was excited to show off my very responsible deed.

Mom, Dad, and Milo curiously made their way to the laundry room. When they got there, I proudly gestured to the basket of folded clothes, then patiently waited for them to thank me. That's when I noticed the looks on their faces. They were not happy looks.

"My soccer shirt!" Milo screeched, yanking it from the laundry basket. "It's pink!"

"Hazel, you washed my wallet!" Dad shrieked, taking a bill-fold from the pocket of a pair of jeans.

"What's this?" Mom asked, holding up a piece of fabric between two fingers.

I told her it was her wrap dress.

"WHAT?" she replied calmly (okay, more like howled furiously).

Apparently, it was three sizes smaller than before I'd washed it. (It looked to be about $\frac{1}{59}$ of its original size, but that's not really the point at this moment in time.)

Did I mention I'd never done laundry before?

13

The next day, Thursday, my family was still so angry about the laundry incident that I was actually happy to get to school. That is, until Mrs. Agnes pulled me aside.

"So, Hazel," she said. "How's the planning for Pet Day going?"

I wanted to tell Mrs. Agnes that it wasn't "going" at all because I'd been kind of busy trying to prove to my family that I was responsible by doing things like laundry, which ended up being a total disaster but was partly my dad's fault because he hadn't stopped with the power tools for *days* now and it was driving me nuts, especially because it was for my dumb brother's loft bed and not for my iguana. But I couldn't tell Mrs. Agnes all of that.

So instead I said, "Oh, fine. Terrific! Coooooouldn't be going better."

Mrs. Agnes tilted her head quizzically. "Do you need help with anything?"

"If you insist," I replied. Because I did, for real live.

Later that morning, I showed Mrs. Agnes my planning guide, and together we decided the first order of business was to divide the class into the following committees: Pet Wash, Fashion Show, Concessions, Pet Portraits, and Entertainment.

Then, during free time, we suggested that everyone meet with their committees, and while they did this I flitted around the room, listening in to their conversations and saying helpful things like "Mmmmmm!" and "Oh yes!" and "Lovely idea!" Suddenly, this team-leader job didn't seem so bad after all. It was actually kind of fun.

Then things took an alarming turn. One by one, my classmates started coming up to me, each with a list of questions. The Pet Wash Committee needed to know what the budget was for buying pet shampoo. The Concessions Committee wanted to know where to order the food from. The Fashion Show Committee asked how many outfits they needed. The Pet Portraits Committee needed a deadline for getting the easels and art supplies.

I was feeling more frazzled by the second. I didn't want to answer all of these questions. I

couldn't answer all of these questions. I just wanted to sit at my desk and design a reading corner for Fred. (And yes, I'm aware that iguanas can't read, but I also know they are very intelligent animals, so who knows what skills he might acquire?) The point is, I turned everyone's questions over to Elizabeth. And also, at that moment I realized I was in way over my head.

• • • • •

By Friday afternoon, my list of Pet Day to-dos had grown to six pages. I had never been so happy for the weekend to come . . . until I

remembered that meant being home with my family, who were all still peeved about the whole "Hazy ruined our clothes" episode.

"Look at my sweatshirt!" Milo bellowed Saturday morning. "It's supposed to be white, and now it's . . . this!" He jabbed his finger at the formerly white sweatshirt, which was now an odd shade of purple and had a bunch of mysterious rough patches all over it (much like an iguana's skin, I wanted to point out, but then thought better of it).

"That's it." Milo glared at me. "You are NEVER sleeping in my loft bed! EVER!"

"Like I ever wanted to!" I yelled back. Even though I kind of did. The truth is, I'd love to

sleep way up off the ground, imagining I'm on a
mountaintop high in the sky . . .

Of course, all of that depended on Dad finishing the bed sometime this century. And by
the constant sounds of drilling, sawing, and
whatever else he was doing in there all weekend long, that didn't seem likely.

By Sunday afternoon, I'd decided that if I
didn't get out of the house soon, I might drill a
hole through the wall myself. So I headed over to
Elizabeth's. And I'd like to say, sometimes being
with your bestest friend is just the thing a girl
needs. For the rest of the day, Elizabeth and I had
a blast. We painted our toes. We practiced our
handstands. We used gum to pretend we had
braces. We sang karaoke. We had twelve rounds
of a staring contest (I won eight, she won four).
It was the most fun I'd had in a long time.

I was about to head back to my house of horrors when it happened: prickles and goose bumps, hot and cold. Then, a tomorrow vision appeared . . . of a fuzzy purple monster and an ice pack.

Now, I've used my share of ice packs, most recently when Milo and I were fighting over who would get the popcorn out of the micro-wave and we both slammed into the kitchen counter. But I couldn't recall ever coming in contact with a fuzzy monster, which I consid-ered a good thing. I certainly couldn't imagine how those two things went together.

When I told Elizabeth, she seemed alarmed.

"How scary! What if a monster is going to sneak into your house? Or school? Or the re-hearsal for my Pet Day performance, which would be totally distracting!"

She seemed most concerned about that last one.

I told Elizabeth we should sleep on it (the tomorrow vision, not the monster), and she agreed, adding that as my sidekick, part of her job was to help me figure out my visions.

I was about to ask her what the other part of her job was, because I don't think we ever ironed that out, but she was on to the next sub-ject. Pet Day.

"Did you call the pet-portrait artist?"

I didn't.

"Are you making the goody bags?"

I wasn't.

"Have you gathered the art supplies so we can make Pet Day posters tomorrow?"

I hadn't.

But *I thanked her for reminding me*, and if that isn't leadership, I don't know what is.

Although I'm sure it's explained somewhere in her planning guide.

14

Monday at recess, I set out paper, markers, and paint that I had *very responsibly* brought from the art room so my class could make posters for Pet Day. Shelby, Lila, and Derrick were creating signs for each station, while Zoe and Deacon worked on a giant banner. I myself was making a poster of a dog and cat frolicking on the beach, and yes, I realized this wasn't entirely accurate since Pet Day was taking place at school, and also because I believe cats have a

negative reaction to waves. But still, I thought it was a pretty good poster.

Suddenly, Elizabeth rushed over to me.

"Hazy Bloom, guess what!" She grabbed my hand and hissed in my ear, "I saw a *fuzzy monster.*"

My eyes widened. "Here?" I said, slightly concerned. I thought that if a monster was approaching the playground, I would have noticed.

She explained, "It's *tiny.* And it's not a real monster. It's a pencil topper!"

"A pencil topper?"

"Yes! And you won't believe who it belongs to."

I followed her gaze across the playground. It was Summer. She was sitting in a circle on the grass with a few kids from her class, jotting away, holding a pencil with—you guessed it—a fuzzy monster on top. First, I wondered where I could get one of those things, since it was totally adorable, for real live.

Second, why would I have a vision about Summer? I mean, because of her amazing luau idea, she *was* my biggest competition for the (not)FUNdraiser. Maybe it had something to do with that? Plus, I hate to say it, but—I just didn't trust her. Perhaps it was because of her extreme snootiness. In any case, I needed to get to the bottom of this. And I had a plan.

"I think we should—"

"Here's the plan!" Elizabeth interrupted.

Fine, we'd go with her plan.

She continued. "Our goal is to get close to Summer, but not too close! Then we can hear what they're talking about without being seen. So you'll sneak through the playground, and I'll sneak through the rotunda. When it's clear to proceed, I'll give you a signal. Like this." She

made some crazy
signal with her
hands that looked
like she was swat-
ting away ten flies.
"When you see that, go
to the front of the picnic
tables but *behind* the slide, and that should get
us close enough to see what's going on!"

I pondered all of this. "Can't we just walk
up to them and ask what they're doing?"

Elizabeth didn't reply, but her look said it
all. We were going with her idea.

We named our mission OPT ("Operation
Pencil Topper"), and after a quick secret hand-
shake, we were off, heading our separate ways
but maintaining eye contact the entire time.

It was kind of fun, in a spy-movie sort of
way, except for the part when I stepped in mud
and my shoe came off. Eventually, we ended up

at our meet-up spot—close enough to hear Summer and her friends talking, but not close enough that they'd see us.

Unfortunately, some other kids had started a game of kickball right between them and us, and with all the yelling back and forth we couldn't hear anything. I began to creep closer.

"Hazy Bloom, what are you doing!" Elizabeth whispered.

But I didn't answer, because I was on a mission, for real live.

A kid from the kickball game scored a point and everyone cheered.

"Switch sides!" he called out.

The two teams ran past each other, almost knocking into me. I dodged out of the way, and before I knew it, I was standing inches from Summer. I quickly turned away, pretending to focus on the game. But now I could hear every word she and her friends were saying.

"Do you really think we can pull it off?" a redheaded girl was saying giddily. "Totally!" another girl said. "It will be hilarious."

My eyes widened. *Pull what off? What will be hilarious?* Something was feeling very wrong about the way they were talking.

"Then it's settled. We'll do it!" Summer said.

I peered over my shoulder and saw her using her fuzzy-monster pencil to write something down in her notebook. "This is going to be the best surprise ever."

I started putting things together in my head. *Pull it off . . . hilarious . . . surprise . . .* It sounded like they were planning some sort of prank. On who? Elizabeth and me? Our class? Or . . . were they planning to do something at

Pet Day? Well, they weren't going to get away with it. Not if I could help it!

I stormed up to Summer. Actually, I was so close that I just kind of turned around. "For your information, I heard what you said," I announced, an edge in my voice.

Summer blinked up at me, clearly surprised. "Oh, hi, Hazy."

"Don't 'Hi, Hazy' me! I know what you're doing, and it's not going to fly!"

"What are you talking about?"

"A hilarious surprise? Pulling it off? You're planning to ruin Pet Day!"

"No, we're not!"

"Yes you are! I know what I heard!"

"Well you heard *wrong*, because we were talking about Mr. Plinker."

"And another thing—" I stopped. "Mr. Plinker?"

"Yes. We're going to ask him to perform at the luau. As a surprise guest. He's a great singer."

I didn't know what to say, so I said, "Prove it."

"That he can sing?"

"No! That that's what you were talking about!"

Summer held up a pad of paper that showed what she had written with her fuzzy-monster pencil. *Mr. Plinker—surprise performer at Luau!* That was proof if I ever saw it.

Summer was now glaring at me. She stood up and looked me in the eye. "You know, I *was* going to invite you to our luau. But now, I'm NOT." She turned to her friends. "Come on, guys."

Mr. Plinker— surprise performer at Luau!

Summer and her friends marched away snootily, glancing back at me and shooting me evil looks. As I was thinking about the fact that I had just eavesdropped on someone and then accused that person of planning to do something they were totally not planning to do, I saw an object slip out of Summer's backpack. It was her fuzzy-monster pencil.

I picked it up and called out weakly. "Hey, Summer, you dropped this—"

And that's when I saw the kickball hurtling

toward me. I tried to duck, but it got me right in the cheek. Hard.

Five minutes later, I was in the nurse's office holding an ice pack to my face. Unfortunately, at that moment my vision made perfect sense.

15

By after school the next day, my cheek was feeling better. So when Mom asked me if I would watch The Baby while she did her yoga video, I said, "Yesireebob!" even though her name is not Bob, it's Theresa. Besides, I was well aware I had some catching up to do in the "showing I'm responsible enough to have Fred" depart-ment. Babysitting was the perfect opportunity.

Ten minutes later, I was very responsibly watching The Baby, who at the moment was spinning in circles, wobbling back and forth, then plopping onto the floor and shouting, "Oopsie!" Then he'd get up and do it all over again. It was hilarious. But after the ninth time,

I told him to stop, because he was definitely going to get hurt (very responsible of me!).

But did he listen? No. He just kept on spinning and plopping.

"Alexander, stop," I said gently but firmly.

"Trabutzblech!" he said back as he bonked into the coffee table.

I reached out and took him by the shoulders. "Hey. *No more.*"

To my surprise, he stopped spinning and sat himself gently on the floor. Then he started throwing blocks.

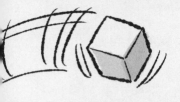

I ducked before one could hit me. "NO! NOT OKAY! STOP!" I yelled.

The Baby looked at me very seriously for a second, then reached out his chubby little hand and squeezed my nose. Hard.

"Ouch!"

That was it. He was going in Baby Time-Out. I scooped him up as he flailed around like a wild octopus, wailing like one, too. Flailing and wailing, wailing and flailing.

"WAAAAAAAAAAAAAAAAAAAAAAA AAAA!"

"Stop it stop it stop it stop it stop it!" I shouted.

Milo flung open his bedroom door. "WHAT IS GOING ON! I'M TRYING TO FINISH MY HOMEWORK BEFORE DAD GETS HOME!"

"Well, *I'm* trying to get this nutso baby to behave!" I screamed at him.

"Well, you're doing a terrible job!" Milo screamed back.

I put The Baby down and glowered at Milo. "That's it. You're in time-out, too."

"You can't put me in time-out! I'm older than you!"

"Like I care!"

"Like *I* care!"

We went back and forth like this a few more times and then suddenly I looked down. "Where's Alexander?"

I scanned Milo's room, hoping The Baby would pop up from the building materials still scattered all over the floor, or from under the mattress Milo had been sleeping on while Dad was working on the loft bed (which still didn't resemble anything close to furniture, in case you were wondering). No baby.

"Alexander?" I called out, panic rising in my chest.

Nothing.

Milo seemed a little freaked-out, too, but he was quick to say our house wasn't that big, so The Baby couldn't have gone that far. This was true, and I momentarily felt some relief. Surely he was around here *somewhere*.

Then I saw that the front door was open. *Uh-oh.*

As we raced down the hallway, terrible thoughts swirled through my mind. *What if he wanders into the street? What if he falls into a ditch? What if he's eaten by a bear?* (And don't tell me there aren't any bears hanging out in the suburbs of Denver. Just because you haven't seen one doesn't mean they're not here.)

Finally . . . FINALLY! We found The Baby.

He was actually just on the front porch. But still, I was enormously relieved. I grabbed him in a big hug (a bear hug, I might say, if I hadn't just imagined him being eaten by one). I'd never been so happy to see him in my life. And I was pretty pleased with Milo, too, for joining me in my freak-out.

Then I realized this might not make me look like the best babysitter. Thinking fast, I scooped up The Baby and ran inside before anyone else could see what had happened.

Mom was standing there. You'd think she'd look peaceful and calm since she'd just finished yoga, but instead she looked on edge and slightly enraged. "What's going on here?" she demanded.

I glanced at Milo, hoping he'd back me up.

"Later," he said, and sped off to his room.

Gee, thanks.

I explained to Mom that I'd simply been on my way to putting The Baby in time-out for terrible baby behavior when he'd had the *nerve* to exit the house without telling me, and thank goodness I was clever enough to find him before he was hurt or eaten, for real live.

I'm not sure what I expected from Mom, but it was along the lines of "Congratulations for your bravery and quick thinking."

Instead, she said in a very serious tone, "You let The Baby leave the house?"

"Of course not!" I said. "He left by himself."

"WHAT?"

Mom told me to go to my room and that I was punished for the rest of the night.

I didn't even get a thank-you for possibly preventing a bear attack.

16

To make up for the Great Baby Escape—and also since I wasn't allowed to leave my room on account of being punished—I decided to do my homework early and then use the rest of the evening to work on Pet Day.

I took out some blank paper and was about to make the Pet Day schedule that everyone had been bugging me about, but my mind started wandering (not my fault!), and suddenly, instead of writing down a detailed hourly schedule, I found myself sketching an elaborate obstacle course for Fred. I know I shouldn't have let myself get distracted, but on the bright side, it was a really cool obstacle course, for real live.

I was almost finished with the last part—an extra-high climbing wall (don't worry, iguanas can survive falls of up to fifty feet without sustaining injuries)—when the prickles and goose bumps came. Another tomorrow vision.

Still holding my pencil, I scribbled down

what I saw, even though it was hard to tell if they were letters or numbers. *SOZ?* . . . *5OZ?* . . . *5O2?* . . . Then, two vertical dots appeared, and suddenly, it made sense: 5:02. As in, the time.

Would something be happening at 5:02 tomorrow? What could possibly be going on that

early in the morning?
I needed to find out.
That night before bed, I
set my alarm for 5:02 a.m.
Then I reset it for 5:00 a.m.
so I'd have a couple of minutes to prepare.
For what, I had no idea.

• • • • •

If you think it's easy waking up at five o'clock in the morning, let me break it to you—it's not.

As my alarm clock blared and I fumbled for the button, I knocked over my lamp, which fell onto a cup of water, which spilled onto my head, which caused me to topple out of bed and onto the floor. At least the heap of clothes (which was now taking up about $9/10$ of my room) cushioned my fall.

I sat up and rubbed my eyes. Groggily, I stared at the clock as it flipped from 5:00 to 5:01, and then from 5:01 to 5:02. The time from my vision. I didn't know what I expected to happen, but here's what I did not expect: nothing. I thought for a second. Maybe it—whatever *it* was—would be occurring somewhere else in the house?

I stood up, still sluggish, and made my way to the living room (well, after stopping in the kitchen to grab some yogurt—if I was up this early, I figured I might as well eat something).

In the living room, I looked around expectantly.

Nothing.

I peeked out the window into the backyard.

Zilch.

I crept into Mom's office and glanced around.

Not a thing out of the ordinary.

Seriously, if I'd gotten up this early for

nothing, I was going to be super annoyed, for real live.

Then I heard a noise outside Mom's office door. I whirled around, grabbing a pencil off her desk for self-defense. True, the pencil was unsharpened, so I'm not sure how much it would have protected me, but it was better than nothing.

I heard the noise again. I gulped, a little scared. Then I made my move.

¡AAAAAAA!!!!!

I lunged through the office door with a se-ries of karate kicks and ballet spins that I'd learned one summer in camp. I waved the unsharpened pencil menacingly, and then, from around the corner ... Mr. Cheese ap-peared.

"Aah!" I screamed in surprise, which caused the dog to start bark-ing madly, which caused The Baby to wake up and start screaming his head off.

Within seconds, Mom, Dad, and Milo were awake and hollering and running down the hallway, demanding to know why all this commotion was going on before the sun was even up.

17

Breakfast that morning was not pleasant. Everyone was cranky from being woken up at the crack of dawn, and they didn't even care when I told them I'd had a really good reason for getting up so early, for real live, and if I could tell them what it was, I would, but I couldn't, so they shouldn't blame me for all this hullabaloo. But instead of asking me where I'd learned such an impressive and sophisticated word like *hullabaloo* (a YouTube video about persnickity cats), my entire family ignored me in anger. Even Mr. Cheese seemed furious.

The rest of the day was no better. At school, I was so tired from waking up early I could barely focus.

During art, I put my markers away in the tissue box.

On my math worksheet, I wrote my name so messily that Mrs. Agnes had to ask who "Hyzla Bglem" was.

At lunch, I put ketchup on my bologna sandwich (which actually wasn't half bad but made me queasy afterward).

At recess I tripped and fell. While I was standing still.

By the time my class had gathered for our Pet Day meeting after school, which I had totally forgotten about until Elizabeth reminded me at the last minute, I felt like a zombie but worse, because zombies are dead and therefore do not get exhausted. Trust me, I've been forced to watch way too many Halloween movies with Milo. I know zombies. So when Elizabeth suggested we start by going over the list of donations we still needed, I flatly told her I was in no mood.

Who knew "I'm in no mood" would result in a ten-minute lecture on world leadership and human suffering?

"Did Martin Luther King Jr. say he was in no mood to fight for civil rights? Did Eleanor Roosevelt say she was in no mood to stand up for women? Did Mrs. Buttonwaller say she was in no mood to get in her car and drive to work every day?"

I blinked. "Who's Mrs. Buttonwaller?"

"My tap dancing teacher!"

I sighed. I wasn't sure I'd put tap dancing in the same category as fighting injustice and shaping American history, but I understood her point. Like it or not, I was the team leader. I needed to lead.

I sat up straight and shook my arms out. I could do this. I just needed to concentrate for twenty minutes until the meeting was over, and then . . .

"HAZY BLOOM, WAKE UP!"

Oops. I must have fallen asleep. I knew this because Elizabeth was shaking me like a rag doll and also because I'd had a strange, quick dream about me, Martin Luther King Jr., and Eleanor Roosevelt at a tap-dancing convention.

The point was, by the end of the meeting, I realized how much there still was to do for Pet Day and how little time was left to do it. I tried giving myself a little pep talk. *You can do this, Hazy Bloom. You can handle whatever comes your way! Every cloud has a silver lining! There is light at the end of the tunnel! The sun*

will come out tomorrow!
There are plenty of fish in
the sea!

I think that last one has
something to do with getting
married, but still. It worked.
By the time I got home after
the meeting, I felt good. Exhausted, but good.

Then Elizabeth called. "You *did* confirm the
pet-portrait artist, right?"

Gah! Well, that didn't last long.

With the final remaining ounce of energy I
had (about $\frac{3}{100,000}$ of my usual amount), I dialed
the pet-portrait artist and left a calm, profes-
sional message.

"HithisisHazyBloomandItotallymessedup-
forreallivebutcanyoupleasedopetportraitson-
Saturdaythankyou!"

Fine, maybe it wasn't so calm and profes-
sional. But at least I did it.

I sat down at my desk, determined to do as much Pet Day planning as possible before dinner, but I was so tired I had to hold my eyes open with my fingers. As I did this, I saw my clock, which was still on the floor from this morning when I knocked it over. It was blinking up at me from the heap of clothes. Then my stomach lurched.

The clock said 5:02.

At that exact moment, Dad came into my room, holding the phone. It was for me. I hadn't even heard it ring.

"Hello?" I said.

It was the pet-portrait artist calling me back. She was sorry, but she wasn't available. Unfortunately, I had called too late.

So I'd been right. Something *did* happen at 5:02. The pet-portrait artist called me with the worst news ever. I was just wrong about *which* 5:02. It was 5:02 p.m., not a.m.

I flopped down on my bed and started furiously pounding on my pillow. I was still terrible at my tomorrow power, just like I was terrible at planning this fundraiser and terrible at being responsible. Terrible at everything.

And right now, there was absolutely nothing I could do about it. So I did the one thing I had been wanting to do since 5:03 this morning.

I went to bed.

18

"Goooooooood morning!"

I gleefully skipped up to Elizabeth at the bus stop. You might be wondering why I was so happy, since as of yesterday, I was a failure as a team leader, a loser at home, and my iguana dreams had pretty much gone down the drain, or down the tubes, or whatever happens to dreams when they are yanked away from you forever.

But you know what? I'd gotten twelve hours of sleep, which hadn't happened since I was six years old. And I felt great!

"Hazy Bloom, what's with you?" Elizabeth demanded. "Why are you so happy?"

"What, is being happy against the law?" I said, slinging my arm around her shoulders just because.

"No," she replied, which wasn't necessary, because I already knew the answer. I explained to Elizabeth that I felt rested and refreshed, and I was ready to lead our class to FUNdraising victory!

"And how are you planning to do that?" she scoffed. "Have you looked at your planning guide lately? No, you have not!"

"I have *too*!" I snapped, completely offended. I reached into my backpack to take out the planning guide and prove to her how much I'd been looking at it. But it wasn't there.

Then Elizabeth held it up. "You left it at my house. It's been there since Sunday."

Oops.

I took the notebook from her and flipped it open to my to-do list. There were about twenty-five things still to do! And that was just page one. My cheery mood was quickly spiraling into free fall. How was I going to do all of these things by *Saturday*? That was two days away. There was no way. No way!

At school, my classmates were bombarding me with last-minute problems: We needed more costumes for the fashion show. We needed more treats for the goody bags. We didn't have enough drinks. We needed extra buckets for the pet wash.

I also still needed to find a pet-portrait artist.

Meanwhile, everywhere I turned—in the hallway on my way to lunch, at the water fountain, in a bathroom stall—I was forced to look at the beautiful posters for the Lipkin Luau. Even Summer's handwriting seemed snooty.

I couldn't even discuss last-minute Pet Day planning with Elizabeth at lunch because I was still being forced to sit with Mapefrl, who was still working on his Burp Man comic. It was still really dumb. Although I was kind of impressed by how well he

drew the Burpmobile. Very impressed, in fact. When I really looked at it, I could see that he had added a lot of interesting detail, and the vehicle actually looked like it was taking off into flight. *Stop it*, I said to myself. *You should not be focusing on Mapefrl! You have a fundraiser to plan!*

But I was losing hope. I didn't know how we'd ever be ready for Pet Day by Saturday. Mrs. Agnes had offered to help, but I didn't even know where to tell her to begin. I kind of felt like giving up. I was a team-leader failure.

After school, I plodded into my house and hung up my backpack, expecting to hear Dad's power drill of doom. But I didn't hear anything. Instead, Dad was in the living room waiting for me. Mom was there, too. They wanted to talk.

Uh-oh.

19

As I sat down on the couch between Mom and Dad, I searched my brain trying to remember what I might be in trouble for. Unfortunately, there were many options: eating The Baby's breakfast, calling Milo a chicken butt, forgetting to do my science homework, using Mom's important papers to make an origami iguana. The point is, the chicken-butt thing was totally Milo's fault because he started it. Anyway, I knew I was probably in trouble for one of those reasons. Maybe all of them. Based on how my life was going, I wouldn't have been surprised.

I braced myself for the lecture.

"Hazel," Mom began slowly, "we know you've been wanting an iguana for some time now."

Oh no. It was worse than I'd thought. They were going to tell me I couldn't get Fred. Ever. They'd decided I was the most irresponsible person in the history of ever, even though it's not my fault the laundry shrank or The Baby ran out the door or the plate JUMPED out of my hands and broke itself on the floor, or . . .

Okay, fine. It was my fault. All of it.

"So Mom and I had a chat . . . ," Dad continued.

Were they still talking? What was the point? They should just come right out with it: *You're never getting an iguana, and to punish you for all of your irresponsible behavior, we're making you change The Baby's poopy diapers every day, forever—*

"Hazy, are you listening? Did you hear what we said?"

I looked up.

"We're getting you an iguana."

WHAT?

I stared at Mom and Dad as if they were playing a huge prank on me and any minute they'd say *Gotcha!* But they were smiling in a very nice and non-pranky way.

"I don't understand," I said. "What about all that stuff I did wrong?"

Dad pulled me onto his lap. "Here's the thing, kiddo. We know you've been doing your best to show us that you're responsible. And it's true, things didn't always go the way you'd planned. But we noticed how hard you were trying. And that counts for something. Actually, it counts for a lot."

"We're proud of you, Hazel Basil," Mom added. "And we know you'll take great care of an iguana."

"I will! I really, really will!"

I could not believe this. I was getting an iguana! I was getting Fred! I hugged Dad, maybe a little too tightly, and then I jumped over to Mom's lap and hugged her, too. "Thank you, Mom! Thank you, Dad!"

"You're welcome, honey," they both said, laughing.

Then I asked, "When can we go to the pet store?"

They looked at each other. "How about to-morrow?"

I could hardly wait.

20

The next day, we went on a family trip to Critter City. Milo took The Baby to look at the kitty cats while Mom, Dad, and I followed the salesperson over to the reptile section. I peered into a giant cage, where about ten iguanas were

scurrying around, playing, drinking, sleeping, waiting to be adopted. I couldn't believe the time had finally come.

"So, Hazel, who's the lucky lizard?" Dad said playfully.

I was trying to decide between one iguana who looked confident and brave and another who looked shy yet feisty when something caught my eye. The same salesperson from before was now setting out a bunch of items in two big bins labeled CLEARANCE.

Even from far away, I could tell that one bin was filled with dog costumes.

"Just a sec, Dad," I said.

At the bins, I picked up a doggie tutu, a tiny sweater with candy canes on it, and a giant bow tie. They would be perfect for the Pet Day fashion show. In the next bin, I found a pink vest and a fireman's hat. I started grabbing stuff. Lots of stuff. Then I saw that near the costume bin was a tray of dog treats, along with some toys filled with catnip. I scooped up some of those, too. Then I grabbed some squeaky toys, including a few that were shaped like trophies, and a couple of bottles of pet shampoo. Soon my arms were so full, the salesperson had to rush a shopping cart to me so I didn't drop everything.

Mom and Dad walked over.

"Hazy? What are you doing? What about the iguana?"

They were looking at me curiously, unsure what was going on.

And then I said something I never thought I'd say in a million zillion years: "I don't want to get an iguana today. Can I get this stuff instead?"

At first, Mom and Dad looked like they might rush me to the doctor, because clearly I was losing my marbles. But I found myself explaining to them that I really needed all of these things, because Pet Day was *tomorrow* and there was so much to do, and I was team leader, after all, which was a job I took very seriously, for real live. Suddenly, Mom and Dad had these goofy, proud expressions on their faces, but I couldn't pay much attention, because I had just spotted the cutest tiara that I *had* to get for the winner of the fashion show.

The car ride home was different

than I'd expected. I thought I'd be sitting in the back seat with Fred and a month's worth of iguana pellets. Instead, I had six huge bags of stuff for Pet Day.

And I couldn't have been more excited.

21

Two other things happened on the way home from the pet store. The first was that I got another tomorrow vision. This time, it was of a bunch of purple spaghetti dancing across the floor. And yes, I realized this is not something you see every day, or probably ever, but I didn't have time to think about it, because I had a long night ahead of me and have learned the hard way that I can only concentrate on one thing at a time.

The second thing that happened was Aunt Jenna called. Since she rang Mom's cell phone, and since I was in the back seat surrounded by all my Pet Day supplies, I asked if I could call her back when I got home. But Mom hung up and told me Aunt Jenna just wanted to wish me luck for Pet Day, which I thought was very nice of her. Then I realized something.

"Mom, did you tell Aunt Jenna about Pet Day?" I asked.

"No, I didn't."

Neither had I.

• • • • •

I spent the entire night sorting, labeling, arranging, and coordinating for Pet Day, which included creating fourteen different outfits for the pet fashion

show. Then with Elizabeth's help, I counted the snacks and drinks for the concession stand, checked all the supplies for the pet wash, and filled every last goody bag with yummy pet treats. I called Mrs. Agnes and asked her to send an e-mail to our class to make sure they knew where to go, what time to be there, and what last-minute items to bring. And thanks to Elizabeth's planning guide keeping us on track, by bedtime, I had completed every single task on the to-do list.

Except—I realized with dread—for one thing. I'd never found a replacement artist for the pet portraits. I knew how excited everyone was about having

their little Fido's portrait done. And now there was no one to do it. Just when I'd thought I had everything figured out, it turned out . . . I hadn't. What was I going to do?

Then it hit me. Because suddenly, I knew the perfect person to ask.

I picked up the phone, dialed, then as soon as he picked up, I spoke: "I need you to do the pet portraits, because you're really great at drawing and this doesn't mean we're friends, it just means I think you're a good artist and need your help, okay?"

At the other end of the line, Mapefrl said, "Okay."

$$\bullet \ \bullet \ \bullet \ \bullet \ \bullet$$

Saturday morning, with Milo and Dad holding about a dozen boxes of supplies, I arrived at the school parking lot for Pet Day. Because of

Mrs. Agnes's e-mail, my classmates were there on time and got right to work setting up the stations, hanging signs, and getting everything ready. Meanwhile, I finished up some last-minute business, such as testing the microphone. I figured since I was team leader, I'd also have the job of announcer, which I was absolutely ready for.

"WELCOME TO . . . whoa, too loud! Welcome to . . . why can't I hear myself? Hello? Testing? Hello?" I squawked into the microphone, causing an obscene amount of feedback that made everyone wince and cover their ears.

Elizabeth appeared next to me. "Let me try," she said, and took the mic. She cleared

her throat and spoke.
"Friends, family, pets.
We are honored that
you've joined us on
this very special day!
We have so much fun
in store for you, so
grab a goody bag,
explore the stations,
and have a PAW-tastic
time at Pet Day!"

I gave Elizabeth the announcer job. Mainly because I had many other very important things to do as team leader. But also because Elizabeth was the best announcer I'd ever heard, for real live. What can I say? She has a gift.

Right before it was time for the event to start, I set out a cash box on the entrance table. I had a feeling it was going to be a great day. Assuming it wasn't ruined by a bunch of dancing purple spaghetti.

I rolled my eyes. Even when I didn't want to think about my visions, they had a way of creeping back into my brain.

"Hazel, everything looks wonderful!" Mrs. Agnes ran up to me, clutching a leash. And attached to that leash was an absolutely adorable terrier. I guessed this was Pookie.

I bent down to scratch behind his ears.

Mrs. Agnes continued, "Are you ready? The doors are opening in one minute! One minute!" I wanted to point out that there weren't any doors to open since we were in the school parking lot, but I knew what she meant.

I looked around: The decorations were up. The stations were organized. The signs were hung. All $^{23}/_{23}$ of my classmates were in their places. "Everything's completely and totally ready!" I said, smiling from ear to ear. Because you know what? It was.

22

Do you know how cute animals look in costumes?
Very, very cute.

As each pet pranced down the runway
(five dogs, two cats, one guinea pig, and a fer-
ret) for the pet fashion show, everyone oohed
and aahed and clapped in delight. It was a huge
success. I personally think it was due to my
edgy yet wearable choices of outfits, but the
cuteness was a factor, too.

Even Mr. Cheese was in the show! He wore a top hat and had a tie around his neck, which was charming until he started to eat it. He's still a dog, after all.

And guess who won the prize for Most Fashionable Pet? Pookie! Mrs. Agnes was so proud.

Shelby and Derrick did an amazing job at the pet wash, giving the animals soapy baths and adorning each one with a cute little bandanna afterward. The concessions were selling like crazy, especially the dog treats and catnip. May and Zoe had even set up a little fenced-in area for small pets, which drew an adoring crowd.

And judging by the long line and the happy faces afterward, the pet portraits were terrific.

I have to admit: Mapefrl did an incredible job.

Finally, and perhaps most importantly, there were no purple dancing spaghetti attacks whatsoever. Which was obviously a huge relief. For me, at least.

Throughout the day, I collected dollar after dollar, taking care to put all the money safely in the cash box. I couldn't wait to see how much we had raised. I had a feeling it was going to be a lot. We were totally going to win the fundraising challenge. Or I should now say, FUNdraising Challenge, because you know what? It actually *was* fun!

Sure, I wish Fred had been there to see it all. But the truth is, I might be over the idea of getting an iguana, after all; maybe I'll turn my attention to fashion design.

"Hazy Bloom," Joanna said, coming up to me and waving a ten-dollar bill. "Do you have change? We're about to sell the very last dog cookie."

"Sure. Let me get the cash box." I walked back over to the donation table, where I had expertly hidden the cash box in a little nook under the top.

I reached under to grab the box and my stomach flipped. It wasn't there. I dropped to my hands and knees and started looking around. A shaggy black-and-white husky came up to me, wagging his tail. He probably thought I was playing a game,

but I wasn't. I was having a panic attack because the cash box was gone. I started darting around the table, my heart beating out of my chest. Where was it? *Where was it?*

"Hazy Bloom, are you okay? What's wrong?" Elizabeth looked at me with concern.

I stood up, my eyes filled with dread.

"We have a problem," I said. Then I burst into tears.

23

A few minutes later, Elizabeth had calmed me down by making me sit in a chair, take fifty deep breaths, and visualize a taco, and while I didn't understand that last part, surprisingly, it worked.

When she saw that I was better, she said, "Okay, let's just think about this. Where did you last see the cash box?"

"Right there!" I gestured emphatically at the table.

"Are you sure you didn't take it anywhere else?"

"I'm sure! I'm definitely, positively, absolutely—oh wait."

I had just remembered: I'd grabbed the cash box on the way to the fashion show so it would be safe. Then I took it with me to the pet wash. And the pet portraits. And the concession stand when I got a hot dog.

This was so not fair. By trying to be extra-responsible, I ended up being *not* responsible about the most important thing in the world.

"What am I going to do?" I lamented. "All of our money is gone!"

I slumped down to the ground and began thinking about which deserted island I would escape to now that no one in my class was ever going to talk to me again, when Elizabeth turned to me intensely, as if something had just occurred to her.

"Hazy Bloom, did you have any visions yesterday?"

This comment made me think that either a) Elizabeth had a very short attention span or b) she was changing the subject to make me feel better. But then I realized it was neither of those things. She was looking for a clue.

I told Elizabeth about the dancing purple spaghetti. At first, she looked completely bewildered, which I understood, because believe me, I'd had the same reaction. Then she asked if there was something . . . *anything* else I remembered.

I squeezed my eyes closed, trying as hard as I could to "re-see" my vision. "I remember seeing something yellow . . ."

"Yellow?"

"There were two of them. Two yellow . . ."

"Two yellow what?" Elizabeth practically shouted.

"I don't know!" I said, my eyes still closed. "I couldn't tell!" I squeezed my eyes tighter, willing my memory of the image to come into focus. "Bananas? Sticks of butter?" I paused. Was that a logo? "Shoes?" I said. My eyes flashed open. "They're yellow sneakers!"

"Sneakers!" Elizabeth exclaimed.

I frowned. "But why would sneakers have purple spaghetti on them?"

Elizabeth thought about this. Then she smiled. "Tell me, Hazy Bloom. What's long and squiggly and goes on shoes?"

"Oh right. Like something like *that* exists."

Then my eyes opened wide.

"*Shoelaces!*" we said at the same time.

Elizabeth and I raced through the masses of people and pets, searching high and low for yellow sneakers with purple shoelaces. It seemed like the crowd was suddenly ten times bigger than before, which was great, because that meant we were getting record numbers, but also terrible because it was really hard to find what—or who—we were looking for.

Just when we were sure we'd searched every foot in the entire parking lot, I spotted them. A pair of very cute, bright yellow sneakers with purple shoelaces skipping through the crowd, causing the laces to bounce and "dance" all over the place. And guess whose feet they were attached to?

Summer's. Did *she* steal our cash box? That thief!

Elizabeth and I rushed up to her. It turned out that she had brought her puppy, too. How dare she bring her pet to our FUNdraiser and then steal our money!

"Hi, Hazy. Hi, Elizabeth. I've been looking for you. Pet Day is amazing. Bruno and I are having a blast."

But before I could say "Never mind that, bub. Hand it over!" like a police officer in the movies, Summer continued.

"Oh! I found this on the ground over there by the concession stand." She held up the red cash box. "Isn't this your money box?"

So, Summer wasn't trying to steal our money?

"You just . . . found this?" I asked.

"Yes. Just a minute ago."

"And you were going to give it back?"

"Of course!"

Well, this was unexpected.

"Thank you," I mumbled. Then I said more loudly, "Really. Thanks, Summer." Summer smiled. And I smiled back. Because that's when I realized Summer wasn't so snooty, after all. She was actually kind of nice. And her puppy was pretty cute, too.

24

That afternoon, after Pet Day was over and we had cleaned, sorted, returned, and swept up every single pet-related item, I stopped by Ms. Simone's class's car wash to show my support. Then that same night, even though a) I was exhausted, b) my throat hurt from having talked all day, and c) I still smelled like dog even after two showers, I went to the Lipkin Luau. Elizabeth came with me, of course. And it was amazing. The school cafeteria had been completely transformed into a tropical island with tiki huts, inflatable coconut trees, and even real sand! We entered the limbo contest. We made our own grass skirts. We drank pineapple smoothies. Elizabeth even joined the hula dance-off . . . and won first place!

Summer seemed so excited to see us. She thanked us for coming, and then said again how much fun Pet Day had been.

Which I kind of already knew, but I thanked her anyway. Then the three of us grabbed hands and ran for the photo booth.

· · · · ·

The total amount of money we raised on Pet Day? Seven hundred sixty-one dollars and two cents. The total combined amount raised by the other two classes was $631, which, if you were good at math (like I am now), you would know is less. So we won!

But honestly, I didn't even care that much. I mean, don't get me wrong. My entire class had been singing my praises all day, which I enjoyed very much. They had even decided I should be in charge of the end-of-school class-awards ceremony (which I declined, and Elizabeth happily accepted). I was just so relieved it had all worked out. And more than anything, I was proud. I had led my team to victory. It turned out I was a pretty good team leader, after all.

At morning assembly that Monday, the principal presented our class with the Lipkin FUNdraising Challenge Trophy. I went up on the stage to accept it and announced that as a class, we had decided our money would go toward improving the reptile section in the library, which was my idea. I felt I owed that to Mrs. Fowler. And to Fred. I had just walked off the stage and was passing the trophy around to my friends when I suddenly felt it: prickles and goose bumps. And then, a tomorrow vision appeared . . . of the Eiffel Tower.

That night, Mom made my favorite dinner to celebrate my victory: spaghetti. Regular colored.

In a fun twist, we were eating in Milo's room to celebrate the fact that Dad had finally finished building his loft bed. Honestly, this was more exciting to me than winning the fundraiser.

And I must say, despite my doubts, Dad did an incredible job. Such a good job that I asked if he would make me a loft bed, too.

Dad told me he'd think about it—after he'd had about a six-month rest.

At the end of the meal, my parents said they had an announcement. The two of them were going on a vacation. I gently reminded my parents that they had three children and asked what we were going to do while they were gallivanting around on vacation and did they just expect us to take care of ourselves, because if someone had to change The Baby's poopy diapers, it wasn't gonna be me.

Mom laughed. "We're not leaving you by yourselves. We'll find the perfect person to come and stay with you."

"Maybe Aunt Jenna can come!" I said. I hadn't thought about Aunt Jenna lately because I'd been so busy with Pet Day. And also, I was